A Blue Bird and Her Little Tree

Copyright © 2021 by Shanghai Press and Publishing Development Co., Ltd.
Chinese edition © 2010 New Buds Publishing House (Tianjin) Limited Company

All rights reserved. Unauthorized reproduction, in any manner, is prohibited.

This book is edited and designed by the Editorial Committee of *Cultural China* series.

Story by Jin Bo
Illustrations by Zhao Guangyu
Translation by Yijin Wert

Copy Editor: Shelly Bryant
Editor: Cao Yue
Editorial Director: Zhang Yicong

Senior Consultants: Sun Yong, Wu Ying, Yang Xinci
Managing Director and Publisher: Wang Youbu

ISBN: 978-1-60220-465-2

Address any comments about *A Blue Bird and Her Little Tree* to:

Better Link Press
99 Park Ave
New York, NY 10016
USA

or

Shanghai Press and Publishing Development Co., Ltd.
F 7 Donghu Road, Shanghai, China (200031)
Email: comments_betterlinkpress@hotmail.com

Printed in China by Shanghai Donnelley Printing Co., Ltd.

1   3   5   7   9   10   8   6   4   2

A Blue Bird and Her Little Tree

A Story in English and Chinese

By Jin Bo & Zhao Guangyu

Translated by Yijin Wert

Better Link Press

A blue bird was flying over the mountains carrying a seed in her beak. Suddenly she heard a soft voice saying, "Please don't eat me!"

The blue bird landed on a barren hill and said, "I am going to plant you here."

一只蓝鸟衔着一粒小小的种子。只听一个细微的声音说道:"请不要吃掉我好吗?"

于是,蓝鸟飞落在一个光秃秃的山丘上,"我把你种在这儿吧!"

The blue bird dug a hole with her beak and planted the seed there. The seed was very happy.

蓝鸟用她尖尖的嘴巴啄啄泥土,把树种埋了进去。种子很高兴。

When spring came, the seed sprouted.

春天来了，种子发芽了。

The seed became a seedling, and soon he became a tree.

嫩芽长啊长,转眼长成了一棵小树。

When the branches were full of flowers, the blue bird flew over to visit her little tree.

"Your flowers are beautiful! Do you still remember me?" asked the blue bird.

枝桠上鲜花盛开的时候,蓝鸟飞来看望她的小树。

"你的花儿真美!你还记得我吗?"蓝鸟问小树。

"How could I ever forget you? You are the one who planted me here." As he spoke, the tree's flowers smelled even sweeter.

The blue bird was very happy. She sang a song for the flowers, then flapped her wings and flew away.

"我怎么会忘记呢,是你把我种在这儿的呀。"小树的花儿开得更香了。

蓝鸟高兴极了,她为小树的花朵唱了一支歌,拍拍翅膀飞走了。

When summer came, the flowers were all gone, leaving the tree with only green leaves. The blue bird came to visit her little tree again.

"Look! All my flowers are gone. Do you still love me?" asked the little tree sadly.

夏天来了,花儿落了,满树只剩下绿油油的叶子。蓝鸟又飞来看望她的小树。

小树有些难过:"你看,我的花儿都谢了,你还爱我吗?"

"Your leaves are also beautiful, " the blue bird said admiringly. The little tree hugged the blue bird with his green leaves.

The blue bird was very happy. She sang a song for the green leaves, then flapped her wings and flew away.

蓝鸟夸赞他:"你的叶子也很美呀!"小树用碧绿的叶子拥抱他的小鸟。

蓝鸟高兴极了,她为小树的绿叶唱了一支歌,拍拍翅膀飞走了。

When fall came, the cold wind blew all the leaves off the tree.

秋天来了,寒风阵阵,一片片叶子随风飘落。

The blue bird came to visit the little tree again.

"Look! I don't even have a single leaf. Do you still love me?" asked the little tree, sobbing.

蓝鸟又飞来看望她的小树。

小树呜呜地哭了:"你看,我连一片叶子都没有了,你还爱我吗?"

The blue bird jumped onto the tree, saying, "Your branches are beautiful, too. When the cold winter is over, you will have your leaves and flowers back! "

The blue bird sang a song to encourage the little tree, then flapped her wings and flew away.

蓝鸟跳上枝头:"你的枝桠也很美呀!严寒过后,还会长出绿叶和花朵!"

蓝鸟为小树的勇敢唱了一支歌,拍拍翅膀飞走了。

When winter came, it started to snow. The little tree did not expect the blue bird to come. He thought she might have moved to the warm south.
But the blue bird came to visit her little tree again.

冬天来了,下起大雪。小树以为蓝鸟不会再来了,她一定会飞往温暖的南方。
但是,蓝鸟又飞来看望她的小树了。

Covered with snow, the blue bird shivered.
"Little Tree, could I build a nest on you?"
The little tree was too happy for words. He smiled broadly.

蓝鸟全身披满了雪花,瑟瑟发抖。
"小树,我在你这里筑一个巢,好吗?"
小树高兴得什么话也说不出来,欢喜地笑着。

The snow grew heavier, turning the whole place white.
The blue bird found a dead branch and laid it on the little tree.

雪真大啊,远远近近白茫茫的一片。
蓝鸟衔来一根枯枝,架在小树的枝头。

From then on, on sunny days, the blue bird flew back and forth, bringing back branches to build herself a nest on the little tree.

从那天开始,晴朗的天气,蓝鸟都飞来飞去,衔回树枝,在小树上筑巢。

On snowy days, the blue bird also flew back and forth, bringing back leaves and feathers for her nest.

下雪的日子,蓝鸟也飞来飞去,衔回叶子和羽毛,继续筑巢。

The little tree enjoyed listening to the blue bird sing during the entire cold winter.

于是,整个寒冷的冬天,小树天天都能听到蓝鸟为他歌唱。

Key Word

Growth

    Children, like seedlings, will eventually grow into big trees. Flowers grow and die, but life always grows stronger. Parents, like the blue bird, will always water seedlings with their love, through the hottest summer and the coldest winter.

关键词
成长

    孩子终将成长为参天大树。无论花开花落，生命永远蓬勃向上。父母仿佛蓝鸟，无论严寒酷暑，永远用爱浇灌幼苗。